DATE DUE

LEGO® CITY ADVENTURES

FIRE TRUCK TO THE RESCUE!

By Sonia Sander
Illustrated by MADA Design

SCHOLASTIC INC.

NEW YORK   TORONTO   LONDON   AUCKLAND   SYDNEY
MEXICO CITY   NEW DELHI   HONG KONG   BUENOS AIRES

ISBN-13: 978-0-545-11543-8
ISBN-10: 0-545-11543-4

40   18 19 20 21 22/0

36 35 34

Book designed by Cheung Tai & Henry Ng
Printed in the U.S.A.
First printing, April 2009

Oh no!
Smoke is in the air.
There is a fire in the city.

B-r-r-r-i-i-n-g!
The fire alarm rings.
The firefighters are on their way.

One by one, they jump into action. They slide down the pole.

9

The firefighters dress in a flash. They grab their hats and boots.

V-r-o-o-o-m! V-r-o-o-o-m!
The fire truck is ready to go.

W-o-o-o-o! Honk! Honk!
The fire truck races down the road.

There is no time to lose.
It is time to fight the fire!

16

Roll out the hoses.
Turn on the water.
S-w-o-o-o-s-h!

Bang! Crash!
Break down the door.
Go fight the fire.

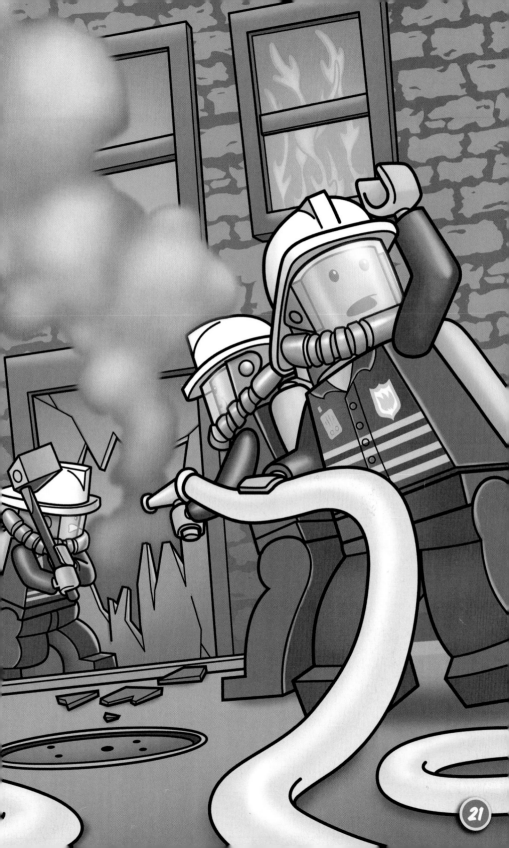

Meow! Meow!
Up goes the ladder. One brave firefighter saves the cat.

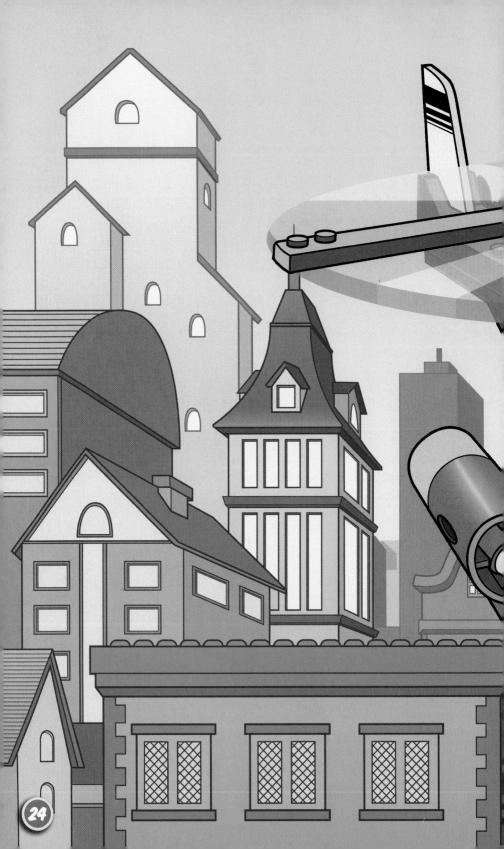

Look high up in the sky.
Here comes even more help.

Water sprays all over.
The fire starts to die down.

At last the fire is out.
The tired firefighters head home.

28

It has been a very long day.
The firehouse is quiet for now.
Only a few soft snores can be heard.

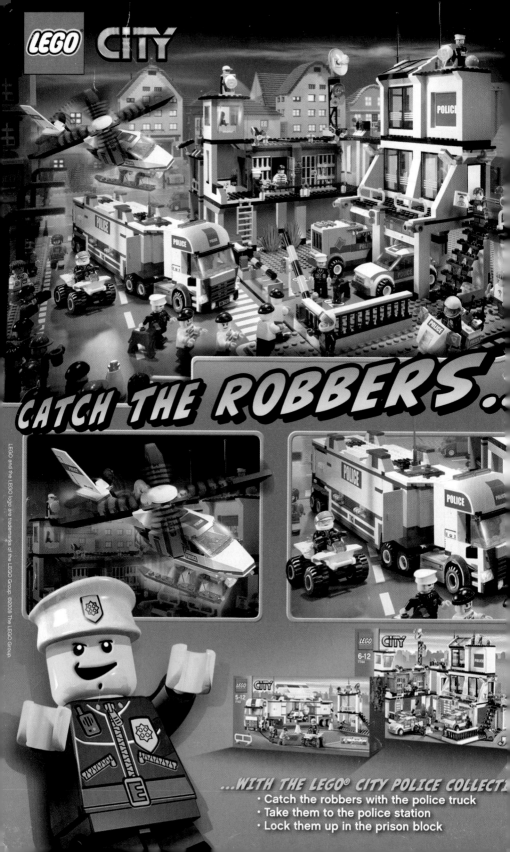

LEGO CITY

CATCH THE ROBBERS...

...WITH THE LEGO® CITY POLICE COLLECTI

- Catch the robbers with the police truck
- Take them to the police station
- Lock them up in the prison block